NIGHT SHOCK

ROBERT GRENIER

NIGHT SHOCK

CHAPTER 1

There were several police cars, a white van with a blue stripe running across its length, and an area taped off with yellow hazard tape in the distance. I drove my car right up to the crime scene, and parked in one of the spots near the edge of the lot. Julia had called me just a moment ago, and I came here as fast as I could. There didn't seem to be any TV news cameramen or newspaper types, though they would be arriving any moment. Exiting the car, I pulled out my P. I. license just in case the cops thought I was a killer returning to the scene of the crime. One of the policemen noticed me, and eyed me wearily as I approached. I held up my P. I. license to eye level.

"Frank Howard Smith, the victim's wife contacted me."

"Keep it on that side of the tape," the cop responded. Private Investigators are no different than journalists or any other civilian to the police. At least I had established why I was here, and hadn't raised any alarms. I was here to observe the crime scene before the police made a mess of it.

On the ground was the body of my friend Kevin McCake, beheaded and heavily burned. Kevin was one of the first people I met when I came to Palm Vista, and I've spent a lot of time with him and Julia over the past couple years. He was a history teacher right at this very spot, the Palm Vista Academy. The taped-off area was at the far end of the parking lot behind the school, farther away from the building than any teacher would park. Someone had discovered the body early this morning and called the cops.

The crime scene photographer was nearly finished, and the coroner was preparing the body bag. In the distance, I saw the Channel 12 news van pull into the parking lot. I wasn't planning to stay much longer, but wanted to see this all with my own eyes. Whoever had murdered him had tried to set the body on fire, but there were a few rain showers last night and the fire must have gone out shortly after the killer left the scene. There was no question that it was Kevin McCake, a small wisp of blond hair had somehow survived the blaze. There was still a horrible smell burnt hair smell in the air. If his ID hadn't survived the fire, the police might have taken days to figure out his identity. Julia said that his phone hasn't been located, but the police are running a trace.

I had seen everything I needed to see, and returned to my car. I was in shock at losing Kevin, he had been a good friend to me and one of the only people I knew in Palm Vista. I knew from experience that I had about an hour before the grief would really set in, and was not looking forward to those emotions when they would eventually arrive. I had told Julia I would come by their house when I was finished here, and it was time to get moving. They lived a few blocks over, and I passed the Channel 10 News van as I pulled onto the street. Kevin McCake would be in the back of the coroner's van by now. His car was nowhere to be seen, but he often walked to work so that wasn't much of a clue. The most confusing part was that Kevin had said that he was going to be in Turkiye this week. He was supposed to be at some sort of archaeological dig on the other side of the world, not dead in his school's parking lot.

It was January, and a cold front had dropped into Florida. The temperatures were down to highs in the upper 40s, which doesn't happen that often. I had a lightweight gray overcoat just for weather such as this, but I probably should have worn a hat as well, I'm now completely bald and get cold easily. I turned on the car's heater, something I almost never do. It felt weird to be wearing a coat in Florida, and I couldn't remember the last time it was this chilly. The roads were mostly empty on the drive over, it was Sunday and the few cars I saw were probably going to or from church.

When I arrived at the McCake's house, Kevin's car was parked in the driveway. There were no other vehicles, which means that the police who notified Julia must have left already. I turned off the ignition and approached the front door, only to have her step through the door to greet me on the porch. Julia looked terrible, her eyes were red from crying, and her expression showed that more tears were soon on the way.

"Frank!" she cried. I gave her a hug, which lingered as she sobbed into my chest. There was no point in speaking, and I hugged her tight. Her tears were coming from somewhere deep in her soul, and her body heaved with grief. I waited for her to signal when the hug should end. A moment later she pulled away, attempting to regain her composure.

"This is terrible," I told her, feeling like I should say something.

"Yeah," she replied, fidgeting with her shirt.

"Did the police say they had any suspects?"

"Yes."

"Which detective is working the case?"

"His name is Muon."

I knew him. Detective David Muon. I wasn't thrilled that it was him, as I worked with him on a previous case that hadn't gone well. A client of mine had been murdered by her ex-boyfriend, and he was the detective in charge of the investigation.

"I've met him before. What did he say?" I asked.

"They have a person of interest. One of his students discovered the body, and she was acting crazy and saying a lot things that made no sense. It also turns out she had a possible motive."

"Motive?"

"She was in Kevin's class and he had failed her for the semester. They said that her dad is a Colonel or something, so they'll probably end up releasing her unless more evidence turns up."

"Did she have an alibi for last night?"

"No. Apparently she was picked up near the school having some kind of breakdown."

"Did the police give you her name?'

"No, they said they weren't prepared to release her name yet. She's a senior at the academy, though. They said she's currently being held at the forensic wing of the psych ward."

Julia invited me inside, and told me she had a pot of coffee on. Normally, I only drink coffee when I first wake up, but my whole morning routine had been shattered by her call earlier. We both went inside, and I headed into the kitchen, where I grabbed a mug out of the cupboard and poured a cup of coffee for myself.

"The cops said that he didn't have his phone on him, whoever killed him probably took it."

"You should put a freeze on his bank account."

Julia drooped her head in frustration. I felt terrible for her. She always had kind of a goth look about her, with dyed black hair and black clothes, which made it all the more painful to see her this deep in genuine grief. I thought she might start crying, but after a moment she tried her best to compose herself.

"I'll call in a little bit. If they opened his banking app the whole account is probably gone."

It seemed wrong to be talking about Kevin's savings, but I didn't want her to have more problems later on.

"When did you last talk to him?"

"Two nights ago. It was early morning over there."

"Did it seem like anything was wrong?"

"No, completely the opposite. He was excited about the dig."

"There were no texts or anything yesterday?"

"No. I was hoping he would call last night, I figured he must have been busy. I think I have to contact the other people that were with him at the dig."

She got a distant look on her face, and I could tell that tears were on the way.

"Julia, I'm so sorry."

"I just don't understand what happened, everyone loved Kevin."

"I know."

I wanted to give her a hug, but wasn't sure if it was the right thing to do. I had already hugged her when I came in, I never know what to do with myself around a grieving person. I was also sad, but my loss paled compared to hers.

"My sister is stopping by in a moment," she said, wiping away a tear.

"That's good," I said. "Listen, I'm gonna head out, but I'll stop by again later."

"Oh Frank, this is so awful," she said.

"I know. Hang in there."

I gave her a goodbye hug and told her I would call her in a couple hours. I went back outside to my car, turned the ignition and put the heater to full blast. I had no idea what to do, and decided that maybe I should just head back to the office.

CHAPTER 2

The downtown area of Palm Vista is not large, being an outer suburb of Miami, and the main strip quickly fades into residential neighborhoods in every direction. My office was only four blocks away, and I began to drive in that direction. After catching a lengthy traffic light, I eventually pulled my blue Mazda 3 into one of the empty parking spaces at the very rear of my building. I entered the building through a side door which opened to a staircase leading to the upstairs apartment.

"Hello!" cried Rory when I entered the apartment. He hadn't been fed yet today, as Julia's phone call this morning sent my day into chaos.

"Hey buddy," I said while approaching the cage. I unzipped a bag of Tropical Bird mix and began loading his food tray. Rory Macaw made a pleased squawk, but didn't say anything that could pass as English. I've been taking care of Rory for three months, and was still deciding whether to keep him. Rory is a Scarlet Macaw who had belonged to a client of mine, now deceased, and I originally took him home out of a sense of guilt. Who knows where he would have ended up.

Julia would probably be busy with her sister for a while, so I put on a pot of coffee and pulled a bagel out of the fridge. I could feel my emotions beginning to catch up with me, and memories from the past year began exploding in my mind.

I thought of the day I first met the McCake's. I was new in town and hired Julia to do my front window sign. Kevin had stopped by with some paint that Julia had forgotten, but he stayed a while to lend her a hand, and since it was about lunchtime the three of us ended up ordering Chinese takeout. Kevin was a history teacher at Palm Vista Academy, and we hit it off talking about ancient Mediterranean cultures. They extended an invitation for me to join them for dinner a few days later, and they soon became friends of mine that I saw at least once a month. This all happened last year, but it feels like I've known them much longer.

I last saw the McCake's about two weeks ago. They invited me over for drinks one evening, and we spent the whole night at their house watching television and listening to music. Nothing seemed out of the ordinary, although Kevin was packing for his trip. He had signed up with some people digging up a burial mound in Southwest Turkiye, and he was planning to write a paper about it after he got back. As far as I knew, he had boarded a plane last week and wasn't expected home for a few more days.

Thinking about this past week, it occurred to me that Christmas break at the Academy probably ended last week, but I think he had scheduled some time-off right after the break. Is it possible he had faked getting on a plane and was in Palm Vista this entire time? It seemed unlikely, but I couldn't rule anything out. It seemed more likely that something happened over there that had him come home early, but why didn't he tell Julia he was back?

I finished my meal, and had no idea what to do with myself. I tried to remember everything Kevin had told me about his upcoming trip. He was excited to be included in the dig, since Turkiye is notorious for not allowing archaeologists to excavate ancient sites. Kevin was invited by a colleague from some organization in Switzerland, and they thought the burial site was from late bronze age. I tried to remember the name of the culture that they were studying, but all I could remember was the Hittites and that wasn't it. I took out my phone and began writing a text to Julia that if she sent me the contact info for the Switzerland group, I could contact them myself. Before hitting send, I thought better of it and decided to just erase the text. She already told me she was going to contact the people from the dig, so I would just have to be patient.

My mind then switched gears to the high school girl that the police considered a suspect. Even though I didn't have a name, I had a decent amount of information. Her dad is a Colonel. Palm Vista does not have a full military base, but there are some administrative offices for the army. All I had to do was find out if there was a Colonel there that had a daughter that matched the description, and I'd have my name.

I went downstairs to my office and sat down at my computer. It took a moment to boot up, but I was soon able to do a search for the words "palm vista florida colonel" and eventually found myself at a staff directory page for the local recruitment center. There was only one Colonel listed, Colonel Lance Gordon. I then typed in "palm vista academy gordon" and landed on a teenager's social media page. Samantha Gordon. The profile photo showed a girl about 18 years old, fair skin, with wavy light brown hair to her shoulders. She looked like a cheerleader, or maybe what we used to call a Valley Girl. The photo was a bit disarming, because this did not look like a killer. I took a moment to scroll through her posts, but she seemed like any ordinary teenager.

I pulled out my phone and looked up the number for the hospital, then dialed. After a lengthy automated recording in which I had to press 4 to speak to a human, a woman answered the phone. I asked what time visiting hours were for the forensic wing, and she said 2-4 and 6-8. I thanked her and hung up.

It was around 11am, and I suddenly wanted to lay down. I felt like I hadn't started grieving Kevin yet, and even though I knew I was still in the denial phase of grief, I was still pretending this wasn't really happening. The full weight of the grief would be coming in waves for the rest of the day. I went upstairs to my bedroom and climbed into my bed. My mind was in a frenzy, but somehow I managed to fall asleep. When I woke up I had the impression that I had dreamed something, but couldn't put it together.

Realizing I might have overslept, I grabbed my phone, and saw that I had received a text message. It was from Julia, telling me that she had emailed the people that were on Kevin's dig to let them know what happened, and that she would contact me when she heard back.

I then noticed the time, and was relieved that it was around quarter to one. I still had plenty of time before the visiting hours, and even though I wasn't really that hungry, I decided to make some instant noodles for lunch. While the water boiled, I did a search to see if there were any stories about Kevin's murder.

All the local news websites now had coverage of it, and I read absolutely every single word I could find. There were very few details, these were just breaking news type articles that are only one paragraph long. None of them revealed his name, only that a body had been discovered near Palm Vista Academy, and that police were investigating.

After reading several of these articles, I added the hot water to the noodles, and then decided to look up where the forensic wing of the hospital was located. I'm glad I did, because it was in a completely different building than the medical center. After I ate the instant noodles, it seemed like it was about time to leave. I got in my car and drove over to the hospital, waiting in the parking lot until it was exactly 2pm.

When I walked through the main entrance of the forensic wing, I was greeted by a woman behind a glass barrier. The barrier had a small opening to pass paperwork through, and also a few small holes in the middle so that people could hear each other speak. I told her I was here to visit Samantha Gordon, and she asked me my relation. I hated to lie, but I said that I was her step-brother. A lot of these places won't let you through the door unless you're immediate family, and the woman asked me for my ID. I slid it through the opening and the woman vanished into a rear office. She came back a couple minutes later with my ID and buzzed the door open for me, telling me to take the elevator to the third floor and to go in the first door to the right. I thanked her and made my way to the elevator.

When I got to the third floor, the first door on the right led to a large room with about a dozen tables. The place was empty, so I sat down at one of the tables near the middle. There were a lot of crayon drawings hanging on the wall, most likely done by patients here. A few minutes later, a young woman that I recognized from the profile photo of Samantha Gordon entered, and looked around with a confused look on her face.

"Samantha?" I asked. She cautiously approached the table, clearly disappointed. I couldn't help but notice that her pupils were extremely dilated, and that she may have done drugs last night, but that otherwise she looked like a normal high school student.

"Who are you?" she finally asked.

"My name is Frank, I was hoping to talk for a moment."

"Did Tommy send you?"

"No, I don't know Tommy."

"Who are you then? When they said my brother Frank was here I assumed it was Tommy using a fake name."

"I was friends with the man that was killed last night."

She recoiled and acted like she was about to head back to her room.

"I didn't kill that guy!" she said, trembling.

Although I just met this girl, I was inclined to believe her. Kevin was brutally murdered, and there was no way this girl did it. This "Tommy" she mentioned could be a person of interest, however.

"I believe you," I replied, hoping to calm her down.

"Look, I already talked to the cops."

"I know," I said calmly. I felt there was a fifty percent chance she was about to flee back to her room, and I had to keep her here for at least a moment. "Could you please tell me what you told them?"

She looked towards the exit, and then back at me. She seemed scared.

"I can try to get you out of here," I added, not sure if that was even the case. Eventually she sat down across the table from me.

"Alright, if it can help me get out of here. Last night I was over at my friend Shelley's house, and she ended up passing out early so I decided to walk home."

She paused, and looked like she was still about to stand up and leave.

"What happened after that?"

"I took the path behind the school because I was trying to avoid this creep who lives in the apartment tower, and that's when I found the body. I called the police but they acted like I was the killer and now I'm here."

"Did you and Mr. McCake have a previous relationship?"

"Eww gross, no."

"I meant you knew him, though."

"Yeah, he was my history teacher." She looked like she might start crying, but I was afraid to comfort her in case she reacted badly. I wasn't sure where to go with the conversation, and decided to change tactics.

"Do you know who could have done this?"

"No," she said, but seemed to be holding something back.

"Not even a tiny suspicion?" I asked, trying to coax something out of her.

"Look, maybe. There's this psycho who's been stalking me, and he and Mr. McCake got into it last week. This freak actually came to my school and showed up at my history class. He got thrown out, obviously. That guy has serious psycho-killer vibes, it was probably him."

"Did you tell the police about this?"

"No. I think the school called the cops."

This wasn't much a clue, but it seemed worth following up on.

"What is this guy's name?"

"John. He lives in that apartment tower by the school."

"Do you know his last name?"

"No. The security guard at the school might, I think they took his info."

We sat in silence for a moment, and I felt like I had bothered this girl enough. I pushed my chair back and stood up. I debated giving her one of my cards. I didn't want anyone to know I was here, but I also wanted her to contact me if she remembered anything else.

"Thank you, Samantha. I'll try to help however I can."

I took out one of my business cards and offered it to her. She seemed reluctant, but eventually took it from my hand. I walked back to the elevator. When I was back on the ground floor, the woman behind the glass buzzed me back into the lobby, and I was soon exiting the forensic ward into the parking lot. It was still chilly outside, but I was feeling satisfied about how that went. I thought they weren't even going to let me in.

CHAPTER 3

Samantha said she thought that the killer was a guy named John who lived at the apartment tower near the school. She didn't know his last name, but said that the security guards at the school might know more. It was a Sunday, and I wasn't sure if anyone would even be at the school, but I thought it was worth a shot. I was going to be driving by the school anyway on my way home, so I might as well investigate.

I drove for about fifteen minutes, and pulled into the parking area for the Palm Vista Academy. At the far end of the lot, I could see that the hazard tape circling the crime scene was still there. The police had left, but three cars were in the parking lot, so I thought there was a chance that a security guard might be around. I parked my car and headed toward the main entrance of the school. The door was unlocked, and I stepped inside.

There was a booth near the entrance where a man in a police uniform was seated. He seemed wary at my presence, and stood up as I approached.

"Hello," I said, "my name is Frank Howard Smith, I'm a private investigator. I was hoping to talk to someone about a man named John who was trespassing at the school last week?"

"I wasn't here last week," the man answered, "but the school principal might know. She's in a meeting right now, and we're locking up after that."

"I can wait," I said.

Down the hallway I could see two people walking our way, an older woman with bright red hair and a tall man in a military uniform.

"Is it alright if I talk to her when she gets here?"

"I'll ask her," he responded.

When the red-haired woman and military man reached the front booth, I could overhear them talking about getting something cleared up. After shaking hands, the military man walked out of the exit without so much looking at me. The man looked pretty high-ranking, and I assumed I was looking at Colonel Lance Gordon. The police officer asked the red-haired woman if she had a moment to speak with me. She seemed hesitant, but soon switched to a more cordial attitude.

"My name is Angela Clarke, I'm the principal of this school. What can I do for you?"

"My name is Frank Howard Smith, I'm a private investigator. I just spoke to your student Samantha Gordon, and she says that a man named John was trespassing on school property last week. She thinks that he's the one who committed the murder here. She didn't know the man's last name, but thought that someone here may have taken it down when he was thrown out of the building."

Mrs. Clarke stared at me for a moment, seemingly on guard for any additional problems that might be coming her way.

"We can speak in my office," she finally relented, "there was a report filed about that incident and I can bring it up on my computer. Once you've filled out a visitor form, of course."

The police officer reached into a drawer and slid a piece of paper my way, and asked me for a photo ID. I showed him my driver's license and my Class C Private Investigator license, just in case there were any doubts about my story. A moment later I was given a small clip-on visitor's pass which I clipped onto my shirt.

"I know it's Sunday," added Mrs. Clarke, "and there are no students here, but I feel better having you sign in. I hope you understand."

I said that I did, and the two of us departed from the front desk into the school. Although the building looks like a normal school on the outside, the interior made you realize that this was a school for the children of rich people. There were tropical plants and marble-looking floors, and I followed the principal up a large spiraling staircase to her office on the second floor. Once inside her office, she slid behind her desk and started to work intently on her computer. A moment later, she turned the screen to face me. It was an incident report from the trespasser last week.

"His name was John Bonito," said Mrs. Clarke. "The police were notified, but I'm not sure if anything came of it."

"Thank you, Mrs. Clarke" I responded. "Is it alright if I take a photo of this report?"

"Yes, that's fine."

I took out my phone and took a quick photo of the screen.

"Were there any other details you remember?" I asked.

"Not really. One of the security guards said he had seen him hanging around a few times."

"Thank you. That's all I needed, I won't hold you up any longer."

"Can you find your way back to the entrance?"

"Yes."

We shook hands and I made my way to the door, and then retraced my steps back down the spiral staircase and followed the hall to the main entrance. I stopped at the front desk to sign-out, and then went outside to the parking lot. The suspect's name was John Bonito, and he lived in the high-rise right around the corner. I have computer software at the office that could probably tell me his exact apartment number, but I thought it might be worth stopping by the apartment building to scope things out.

While the apartment building was only a short walk, I thought it might be best not to remain parked near an active crime scene. I got in my vehicle and drove across the street to the 12-story apartment complex that loomed over this neighborhood. This is where all the low-income and government benefits types tended to live, and I had never stepped foot on the property until today. I pulled into one of the parking spots and made my way to the entrance, which was located on the rear of the building facing away from the street. An older woman was smoking a cigarette near the entrance, but she was the only person in sight.

Next to the main entrance was an enormous push-button buzzer system with four rows of twenty buttons each. There were names handwritten in pen next to most of the buttons, and I quickly scanned the names. The apartment 59 buzzer had the name "Bonito", and I felt a tremendous sense of relief. I pulled on one of the double doors at the entrance and stepped into the lobby.

Ahead of me, I saw a reception desk where a woman was typing away at a computer. She didn't look up as I entered, and I got the sense that people come and go at this place all the time. Guessing that apartment 59 would be somewhere on the 7th or 8th floor, I walked nonchalantly to the elevator and hit the up button. Once inside, I punched the number 7 and tried to act casual as the doors slowly creaked shut. A moment later I was on the 7th floor, and I began to scope for a door with the number 59. Making my way up and down the hallway, it soon became clear that it was probably one more floor up. Seeing a stairwell, I decided to just take the stairs instead of waiting for the elevator again.

On the 8th floor, I found apartment 59 immediately. The door was slightly ajar, and the noise from a too-loud television was pouring out into the hallway. Although I am normally the respectful type when it comes to knocking, the knowledge that the man who killed my friend might be inside made me ignore the usual customs. I quietly pushed the door open, and was greeted with a filthy kitchenette covered in grease and pans that looked like they had never been washed. The television was tuned to a baseball game, and I couldn't believe that someone could watch TV with the volume that high.

"Is anyone home?" I asked loudly, trying to sound official as possible. I didn't come here to perform a citizen's arrest, but I had questions that needed answers. There was no response from inside, and I began to wonder if anyone was even here. I stepped inside, knowing deep down that I was now breaking the law by entering the apartment. My plan was just to look around for any obvious clues, like bloodstained clothing or a possible murder weapon. I stepped through the kitchenette into the living room, but no one was around. Who leaves their TV blaring like this when they're not even home? The place was a mess, whoever lived here was a hoarder. There was a pile of laundry in the corner that appeared to have men's and women's clothing, the table was completely covered in fast food wrappers and cigarette butts, and the place smelled like urine and smoke. Glancing around, I couldn't see anything that was worth alerting the police about.

Without warning, I heard a loud yell come from the bedroom, and a fat crazy-looking guy in a bathrobe was running towards me at full speed. I got half a word out before he body-checked me into the wall and then fled through the still-open front door into the hall. He knocked the wind out of me, and it took a second for me to get back on my feet. I tried to follow him out into the hallway, but I was limping from the attack and I could tell he was gone. This had not gone well.

I walked back to the apartment door and wondered if it was worth going back inside. I decided that I had accomplished enough. I knew exactly what John Bonito looked like and where he lived, and a glimpse into what kind of person he was. He was at least 260 lbs, over six feet tall, more fat than muscular, thinning hair, and pockmarks on his face. That would have to be enough for now.

Despite my injury, I thought I might be best to find a way out of here that did not go past the front desk, since it was likely that he was reporting this incident to the woman working there. I took the stairs down to the first floor, and saw a rear exit leading to some sort of courtyard behind the building. I left through that door, and was pleased to see that I could connect back to the parking lot by circling around. I hobbled around the corner back to my car, turned the ignition, and quickly pulled out onto the street. There didn't seem to be any commotion near the entrance, and I began to wonder if he even spoke to the receptionist about what happened.

CHAPTER 4

I had one more stop I wanted to make before I called Julia. John Bonito lived across the street from the school where Kevin's body was found, but this did not explain why someone who was supposed to be in Turkiye had mysteriously returned. It's possible Kevin was murdered by John Bonito, who may turn out to be some kind of a serial killer, but Kevin also spent the last couple weeks with unknown people in a foreign land. It was too early to rule out someone from out of town.

If this was done by an unknown foreigner, there's a chance that they booked a room at the Palm Vista Hotel. This is where most people stayed when visiting Palm Vista, and it was worth investigating. I had an acquaintance named Dolph who was a bartender there, and he would tell me if anything suspicious happened last night. He normally worked late afternoons to closing time, so he should be there by now. The Palm Vista Hotel was just a few blocks away, and after a short drive, I pulled into the hotel's spacious parking lot.

Entering the hotel, I marveled at how luxurious the lobby seemed. Overhead was a sparkling chandelier, and it was furnished with white carpets with furniture made of white leather. It had its own bar and restaurant in an adjoining room, and everyone was wearing suits and designer brands. There was a young woman at the desk, and I tried to act like I was a guest at the hotel as I walked past on my way over to the restaurant. Dolph was shaking a drink for a customer at the far end of the bar, so I took a seat on one of the stools until he was available. It took a couple minutes for him to notice me.

"Frank, how've you been?" he asked, "Can I get you anything?"

"Nothing right now," I answered, "but I'm a working on a case that may involve this hotel. Did you notice any foreign types here last night, maybe from Turkiye?"

Dolph pondered the question for a moment, but eventually shook his head.

"Nothing comes to mind, sorry." he responded. A second later he seemed to remember something, and his face lit up. "A few men at the bar last night were speaking a foreign language, didn't strike me as Turkish or anything like. Some sort of Eastern European or something, I'm really not that great at languages."

"What do you remember about them?"

"I think it was three guys, they here for a couple hours and then left. I couldn't understand a word they were saying, but they were drinking straight vodka."

"Do you remember anything else about them?"

"No, they left around 10 and that's about it."

"Did any of these three men seem like, for lack of a better word, the criminal type?"

"Honestly? Yes, they kind of did seem like that. We get a lot of businessmen and tourists, but these three seemed like something else."

I handed Dolph my business card. He might already have my number, but I wasn't positive.

"Call or text me if you remember anything else. Also, if you can find out what room they were in, or any of their names, I would owe you a huge favor."

Dolph took my card and slid it into his pocket.

"I'll try, but no promises."

"Thanks."

I said my goodbyes to Dolph and headed back towards the lobby. As I was passing through the lobby towards the exit, I noticed an elderly woman pulling a wheeled suitcase, and one of the compartments was open. Something sparkled on the ground behind her, and it looked like an earring.

"Ma'am, I think you dropped something."

The woman paused and slowly turned around. She saw the earring and bent down to pick it up.

"Thank you, young man. It's good to see that there are still honest people out there, most folks would have just pawned it."

I told her it was no big deal, and started heading for the exit. The woman mentioned pawning jewelry, and this gave me an idea. I'd already had an exhausting day, but I realized I had an additional stop to make before contacting Julia.

St. Vitus Pawn & Collectibles was a place that Kevin had mentioned several times, and I knew that he and the owner Tony had some sort of long-running business relationship. While it wasn't much of a lead, it was worth checking out. It was also located nearby, and somewhat on the way to Julia's place. I had never set foot in the place, but always liked the name. There was once a true story of a strange phenomenon where the entire city of Strasbourg started spontaneously dancing, and many of the people danced themselves to death. They called it the St. Vitus Dance, after the patron saint of dancing. I always found it odd that there was a pawn shop with this name.

When I reached St. Vitus pawn, I parked on the street out front. Getting out of my car and approaching the entrance, I couldn't help but notice that it looked closed. The lights were off, and when I pulled on the front door it was clearly locked. The hours painted on the front door said it should have been open from 11am-8pm. I would have to try back later.

Returning to my car, I pulled out onto the street, but as I was driving past the alley that runs behind the pawn shop I noticed some activity. Traffic was light, so I was able to back up and turn down the alley. Ahead off me was a van parked directly behind the pawn shop, and the rear door of the shop was propped open. I parked and got out of my vehicle, and a moment later someone who was probably the owner Tony exited the rear the door and closed it behind him.

"Hello! Are you Tony?" I asked. He whipped around to face me, and he looked terrified. He was carrying something circular wrapped in brown paper, which he quickly set down in the back of the van.

"We're closed," he said sharply. "We're gonna be closed for awhile."

"I was a friend of Kevin McCake, did you hear what happened?"

Tony slammed the rear door of the van shut, and started to move toward the driver side door.

"I have to leave," he said, looking for a moment like he had a lot more to say. "These people will tie you to a chair and torture you to death."

Tony jumped up into the van and turned on the engine, immediately pulling away. In his own way, he had just given me more information than I even expected. It was time to return to Julia's place and tell her what I had found out. I sent her a quick text, and she wrote back that she was home.

CHAPTER 5

While driving to Julia's house, I realized that things might be rough at her house. She might be sobbing on the floor, or she might have a lot of people over. Either way, I wanted to tell her what I found out, and to see if this information might cause her to remember anything. When I arrived, there were no extra cars in the driveway. I parked and walked up to the door, opening it slightly.

"Julia, it's Frank. Can I come in?"

There was a pause, and I thought I heard her talking on the phone. She appeared around the corner, clearly with her cell phone at her ear. She waved me inside, then returned to the kitchen. I sat down on the couch, trying not to eavesdrop on her conversation. It sounded like she was doing alright, considering the circumstances. Eventually, she finished her phone call and came into the living room.

"How are you holding up?" I asked.

"Not great," she replied. I noticed dark circles around her eyes, and she had clearly been crying not long before I arrived.

"If you want to talk about it, I'm here to listen."

Julia sat down on a chair, and looked defeated.

"I can't believe Kevin is gone," she said. "The last time I talked to him I didn't really say the things I wanted to say. He called from Turkiye, and I was half-watching television the whole time. How was I supposed to know?"

"It's not your fault," I said.

"I told him I loved him before I hung up."

She looked like she was about to cry again. I wanted to tell her about the things I found out that might relate to the murder, but it seemed like a bad time. After a moment, it seemed as if that particular wave of grief had passed.

"I found a few clues this morning,"

"Like what?"

"The student at the murder scene last night is not a promising suspect. There's some kind of psychopath who haunts that area, and I haven't ruled out his involvement. Also, I think there's some bad people in town who may have followed Kevin back from Turkiye."

Julie stared at me for a moment. Even with what I just said, I still felt like I was a million miles away from solving this murder.

"Well, the police are also looking into it. It's not going to bring Kevin back, either way."

She was right, but there was no way I was just going to sit here while his killer was on the loose. The conversation drifted into which of Kevin's friends and family she had been able to contact, and after a while it seemed like she was becoming tired.

"One more thing," Julia said, her face briefly lighting up. "I sent an email to the people that organized the dig in Turkiye. They're in Switzerland, and it's probably the middle of the night there. Still, they might write back or know something."

"That's great. Let me know if you hear back from them."

I stood up, told her to call me for absolutely any reason, and gave her a hug. I was soon on my way back to the car. It was now a little after 6pm, and the sunset had color streaks of coral and violet light. Just as I was sliding in to the driver's seat, my phone started to go off. I didn't recognize the number.

"Hello, this is Frank."

"Hello, Mr. Smith. This is an adjunct to Colonel Gordon. Are you able to take a call?"

I started to feel like I might be in trouble. I had just visited his daughter in the psych ward claiming to be a family member.

"Yes."

"I will patch you through."

A moment later I had Colonel Lance Gordon on the phone.

"Colonel Gordon, I'm sorry I lied to see your daughter. She's an important witness and I had to speak with her."

"It's nothing like that, Mr. Smith. Samantha is home now, she was released into my custody an hour ago. The police do not believe she was involved with what happened. I'm calling about a separate matter."

"What would that be?"

"When my daughter mentioned your visit, she also mentioned that a man has been stalking her. This is the first I've heard of this, and I would like someone to look into this situation."

I debated mentioning that I had already been to John Bonito's apartment, but I decided to keep it to myself.

"I would like to hire you to be at Palm Vista Academy between 2pm and 2:30pm tomorrow, and maybe for the next few days. My daughter says he normally shows up when school is letting out."

"Yes, I can do that. Surveillance gigs are cheap, but I'm assuming that you expect me to get involved if something happens?"

"Money is no object, Mr. Smith. I've already looked at your website and saw your payment information. There will be $500 in your account by the end of the hour."

"Alright. I'll be at the school tomorrow."

"That's not all. I would like you to give Samantha a ride home after school. You are to serve as her security until she is delivered to the house."

"Alright. I'll make sure she gets home safe."

"Very good, I look forward to speaking with you again."

The call ended, and I sat in the driver's seat of my car for a moment to process what had just happened. This was unlikely to help me find Kevin's killer, and would probably be a huge distraction for the next few days. Also, I already knew the stalker's full name and address. On the other hand, I did have bills to pay, and $500 was a lot of money. After idling the car in Julia's driveway for another moment, I decided that it was time to get moving. I pulled out onto the street, turned on my headlights because of the approaching dark, and thought that maybe it was time to head back to the office.

On the drive back, a sense of exhaustion filled my mind. When I finally arrived at the office, I ended up just locking the door behind me and going straight upstairs to the apartment. Rory Macaw did a little dance in his cage when I walked in, and I gave him one of the bird treats I had picked up last week. He made a happy "scree" noise.

This had just been one of the longest days in my entire life, I felt awful, and unless some new piece of information came my way, this whole thing was a bust. I slumped into my recliner, and almost felt myself falling asleep. My friend was dead, and the killer or killers were going to get away

Suddenly, I received a text message. I pulled out my phone and read the text.

"It's Dolph. I tricked the receptionist into telling me the room number. The room was registered under the name Cuiardo. Checked out Sunday at 10am. That's all I could get without the reception password."

I texted him thanks and sat bolt upright. I went downstairs to my computer and got to work. Opening a search engine, I punched in the name I was given and started scrolling through the results. It was clear that Cuiardo is not a common name, and the first things I clicked were the matches on the biggest social media sites. There were only a few profiles with that name, but none of them really jumped out at me. There was a middle aged woman with that last name, a college athlete in Utah, a couple profiles that had no posts, and one guy who lived in Wisconsin who was a huge football fan. I tried to find something that made sense for a killer, but nothing was standing out.

I returned to the search engine and kept scrolling. I noticed an unusual amount of results about Italian poetry, and I guess "cui ardo" had some meaning in the Italian language. Finally, just before the search engine declared that it had run out of results, there was a link to a global directory of art galleries. Clicking on the link, it brought me to an alphabetical listing of every known art gallery in the world, and under the letter "C" was an M. Cuiardo located in Moscow.

I began to wonder why this gallery hadn't show up in my search, but then recalled that they use a different alphabet over there. I used a site to translate Cuiardo into Cyrillic, and then punched that into the search engine. There was an enormous number of results, and I quickly found the website for the art gallery. It was all in Russian, but used the auto-translate option on my web browser to convert it to English.

Slowly, a story began to emerge. There was a gallery in downtown Moscow run by an Italian-born art dealer named Matteo Cuiardo that specialized in antiquities. There was even a photo of him, a slender man with black hair and expensive clothes. I took out my phone and found the website, downloading the man's photo and texting it to Dolph. A moment later, Dolph wrote back that he wasn't totally sure, but that he could have been one of the men at the bar last night.

I felt like I had just solved the murder, but there was no celebration. I had zero evidence. If I called the FBI right now, what would I even say? That the guy from St. Vitus Pawn seemed to know something, and that there were some suspicious Russians in town? However, a picture of what really happened began to emerge. Kevin probably gave something to Tony for safekeeping while he negotiated with Cuiardo, but something went wrong and Kevin was murdered. I needed to talk to Tony. He would be a material witness, but he left Palm Vista in a hurry. I might be able find out where he went, but this would have to wait until tomorrow. It wasn't even 8pm, but I had the type of exhaustion where you are more asleep than awake.

I poured a couple drinks for myself, and spent the remainder of the night mourning Kevin and feeling bad for myself. I've had a tough time making friends since I moved to Palm Vista, and Kevin's murder deprived me of what little social life I had. He was a great guy, and a good friend.

The rest of the evening was a blur. Late in the night I awoke sitting in my chair, not realizing I had even fallen asleep. I moved into the bedroom, and was completely asleep within seconds.

CHAPTER 6

I awoke at dawn. Laying in my bed for longer than usual, I thought I might be able to fall back asleep. I had a headache, and wished I had drank some water before I fell asleep. My phone started ringing, so I grabbed it from the small table near my bed to see who was calling. It was Julia.

"Hello?"

"Frank, it's Julia."

"Good morning. How are you feeling?"

"Like crap. The Switzerland people wrote back."

I sat upright at the edge of the bed.

"What did they say?"

"They said they forwarded my email to the guy heading up the dig, his name is Wilhelm Frederickson. He wrote back to them that they could give me his phone number. He also expressed his condolences for Kevin's death."

"Text me the number. I'll call him and then call you back."

I hung up, and a moment later I had the text with his phone number. I immediately dialed. It rang five times before a man answered.

"Hello?"

The man had an accent that sounded vaguely German or Austrian, and it wasn't clear yet how fluent he was in English.

"Hello, is this Wilhelm?"

"Yes. What can I do for you?"

"My name is Frank Howard Smith. I was given your number by Kevin McCake's wife."

"When I saw the call was coming from America I thought it might be that. I'm sorry to hear about Kevin. I didn't know him well, but he was always friendly to me."

I felt relief that he was an English speaker. Clearly not his first language, but fluent.

"We're just trying to figure out what happened. Did anything happen to Kevin over there?"

There was a short pause.

"I mean, yes and no. Kevin left here last Friday, he said that his mother-in-law had passed and he had to get home."

I knew that Julia's mother had died a few years ago, so Kevin had obviously lied.

"Was there anything that happened, though? Anything suspicious?"

Another pause. I could hear him clear his throat.

"Yes, there was. I got the sense something was bothering him. Things were normal at first, but by the end of the week he began acting odd. He kept wandering off."

"Do you know where he was going?"

"No, we were excavating a tell that had multiple burial layers. He kept saying he needed to clear his head, and would wander down into the valley and disappear for hours. This made everyone feel kind of uncomfortable, and when he announced he was leaving for home it was a bit of a relief."

"One more question. Is anyone on your team from Russia?"

A third pause, this one much longer than before.

"Our society has members from all over the world, including Russia. One of our largest donors is from Russia, and one of his colleagues is part of our team here."

"Does the name Cuiardo mean anything to you."

"No."

I realized I had asked a stupid question. Cuiardo was an art dealer, not an archaeologist. I debated asking him for the name of the Russian donor, but decided I had bothered this man enough.

"Thank you for your time. If you remember anything else, please give me a call."

I hung up, and felt like I had learned something important. Kevin had clearly found something while he was over there, and left in a hurry. I dialed Julia's number and she picked up on the first ring.

"I just spoke to the Wilhelm guy. He says Kevin was acting weird the last couple days he was there, and that Kevin also said he had to fly back to the States because his mother-in-law had died."

Julia let out a long sigh.

"What else did he say?"

"Well, I asked Wilhelm about a couple of things that I turned up."

"Like what?"

"I don't have any solid evidence, but I think Kevin may have crossed some Russians while he was over there, and they may have followed him back to Palm Vista."

"Why do you think that?"

"I talked to the guy at St. Vitus Pawn Shop yesterday, and he said some bad people were in town. I also talked to someone I know at the Palm Vista Hotel, and he said that there were some shady Russians there last night. I even got the name of one of them, and he's a big time art dealer that seems to buy stuff from archaeologists."

"Ok."

Julia sounded stunned, and I worried that if I said anything more, I would be in danger of making her cry.

"Listen, I'm going to get to the bottom of this. I'll call you later."

I knew exactly who I had to get in touch with next, and that was Tony from St. Vitus Pawn. He probably knew everything. After drinking a few cups of coffee, I sat down at the computer and did a quick internet search to get Tony's full name, which turned out to be Tony St. Vitus. I then fired up my skip tracing software and punched in his name. I soon had his address and phone number. He owned a house right here in Palm Vista, but something in my gut told me that he wasn't going to be home for a while. I started going through his social media for clues as to where he might hide out. Unfortunately, he didn't seem to post that often. All I gleaned of interest is that he is married to a Sally St. Vitus.

I ran Sally's name into the skip tracing software, and something interesting came up. She had two addresses listed, the same one as Tony's and a second one a few towns over. I brought up a satellite image of the second address, and it was a small ranch home on a quiet street. I now had both their phone numbers and a likely hide-out. There probably wasn't much point in calling them, there was zero chance of them picking up an unknown number. My best bet was to swing by address number two and see if anyone was home.

I checked the time, and suddenly remembered that I had the Samantha Gordon thing this afternoon. That wasn't until 2pm. It was only 7:30am, so I still had over six hours. Tony and Sally's second address would probably be a forty-five minute drive, which would give me time to scope things out. I'm not much of a morning person, and it was at least an hour before I had my shoes on and was ready to go. I gathered my usual surveillance equipment and headed out to the car. It was still unseasonably cold, and also much cloudier than yesterday.

I got in my car, and was soon on the expressway heading west towards a town I had never visited. It didn't really matter, finding an address in the suburbs was usually a no-brainer. The drive over was uneventful, it started to drizzle, and I had the heater on. I drove in silence for the entire way, it was too early for the radio. Getting off at the exit, I made a few turns, and found the correct street. Checking the house numbers, I decided to pull over a few houses away from the property. I could see Tony's house, and there was a black sedan in the driveway. Someone was home.

I spent a long time watching the house through binoculars, but there was no movement. Although stake-outs are fine for catching a client's spouse in a compromising situation, this was not that type of scenario. I had been sitting in my car for long enough, so I got out of the car and started walking towards the front door, and pushed the doorbell. I listed carefully for any sign of movement in the house, and heard the shuffling of feet somewhere beyond the door.

"My name is Frank Howard Smith, P.I.," I said loudly, hoping to reassure them that I wasn't here to cause them harm. "I was friends with Kevin McCake."

I listened for more movement, but couldn't hear a thing.

"I can slide my ID under the door if that would help," I continued, trying to sound non-threatening.

"Hold on," said a male voice, which I recognized from our brief conversation yesterday. I could hear the door's lock being turned, and soon I was now face-to-face with Tony St. Vitus. He was holding a shotgun, but it wasn't aimed at me.

"Kevin mentioned you before, I guess you're probably ok."

"Sorry to just show up like this," I responded.

"It's alright, come on in."

Tony scanned the street outside after I entered, looking extremely paranoid. He shut the door behind me, turning the lock and sliding a deadbolt.

"So you're Frank," he said. "Kevin was trying to get me to hire you after some trouble I had a few months ago, but I managed to take care of it myself."

"Kevin helped me find a few clients. He was always looking out for people."

Tony sat down in a recliner against the wall. There was a couch in the room, and I decided to sit. The room was sparsely decorated, and I got the sense that they spent more time at their other home.

"I'm just trying to figure out what happened to Kevin," I said, "I've actually got some leads. I'm hoping to discuss a couple things, though."

"Hold on a second," he answered. He stood up and walked towards a side room that looked like a kitchen from where I was sitting. "Honey! It's ok, you can come out if you want. It's not one of the bad guys."

"I'm just gonna stay in here," replied a woman's voice, who I assume would be Sally.

"Suit yourself," said Tony, turning to face me. "So I guess this place wasn't as hard to find as I was hoping."

"Not if you know where to look," I responded. He sat back down.

"You caught me at a bad time yesterday," he said. "I didn't know who you were."

There was an awkward silence, and it looked like Tony was figuring out how much he trusted me. I decided that maybe I should say something.

"I believe Kevin found something on his most recent dig," I said, "and that's what caused this whole mess."

Tony suddenly seemed to tense up.

"Are we safe here? If you found this place than anyone could find this place. I don't know how much they know."

"Do these people know about you?"

"I don't think they do, but I don't want to take any chances."

"I'm only here because Kevin mentioned you to me several times. Do you think he mentioned you to these other people?"

"No," Tony said with confidence, seeming to relax.

"Tony, one of my best friends is dead. Please tell me what is going on."

"Stay here a moment," he said, standing and going to another room past the kitchen. He returned with a plastic crate about the size of a banker's box, and set it down on the floor between us. He took off the lid, exposing layers of bubble wrap. When I saw what was under these layers, I was completely stunned. There was a crystal wheel about 18 inches in diameter, with a hole about 4 inches wide, that was completely covered in strange symbols.

"This is what got Kevin killed," said Tony.

"What is it?"

"We weren't entirely sure, but the symbols look like Luwian hieroglyphs. Kevin overnighted this to me from Turkiye, there was no way he was gonna get it through customs at the airport."

The artifact was incredible. It looked straight out of a fantasy film, but it was real and it was sitting in front of me. I looked at the hieroglyphs which were cleanly inscribed into the crystal, but couldn't make any sense of them.

"What else did Kevin tell you?"

"He called me on Friday, and said that he was shipping me something that could be extremely valuable. He's brought me some good stuff in the past, jewelry, ancient coins, that sort of thing. Nothing like this, though."

"Did he say anything else?"

"Yeah, he and I talked for awhile. I have the whole story of what happened, there is no mystery about who killed Kevin and why."

"Was it an art dealer from Russia named Cuiardo?" I asked.

"I don't know the guy's name. He could be an art dealer for all I know. Maybe I should just start from the beginning."

I tried to signal that he had my full attention.

"So Kevin flew to Turkiye because they were digging up a burial site and he was writing a paper on the Luwians, and he sort of knew the people putting the dig together. After a few days, I guess he got into an argument with one of the people there. Turns out the whole thing was being financed by some wealthy Russian, and he had some of his own guys at the dig."

"I spoke to some Swiss guy who was at the dig, and he seemed alright."

"Oh sure, yeah, but those Swiss people were just being used as cover to get the digging permits. Try to picture a few large mounds all next to each other, though, and about twenty different people digging at different areas. There's no way to keep an eye on everyone, and it's real easy to find something and sneak it off site."

"So Kevin found something and didn't report it."

"It's a little more complicated than that."

Tony paused for a moment, clearly trying to choose his words carefully.

"Kevin started out reporting everything he found. He even caught one of the Russians with some sort of chalice and they almost got into a fistfight about it, at least that's what Kevin told me."

"Where did this come from, then?" I asked, pointing to the crystal wheel in front of us.

"I'm getting there," he said. "Alright, so Kevin liked going for walks, as you probably know."

Tony looked like he recalled something important.

"Wait, let me add something about his argument with the Russian guy. The Russian guy said that his boss had paid most of the expenses for the dig, and that if he got a few artifacts out of it then that was only fair. Kevin told the Russian that he was going to tell the Swiss people about it, and the whole situation escalated. I don't think Kevin ended up telling anyone, though."

"Then what happened?"

"So Kevin was debating just flying home. However, on one of his walks he gets real far away from the dig site, and notices some rocks piled on top of each other in a weird way, and starts to suspect he's found an area of interest. He begins spending more and more time at this site, and less time at the main dig, and next thing he knows he finds this."

Tony gestured to the crystal wheel.

"Since he found it off-site based on his own hunch, he decided that this was his find, and his find alone."

"So he mailed it to you and booked a flight home?"

"Yes, but I wish it were that simple. One of the Russian guys had a close eye on him, like they had a serious problem with each other. Even though Kevin thought he got it mailed without incident, I guess the secret was out. The guy demanded he hand it over and he tore Kevin's room apart looking for it. I'm a little fuzzy on the details, but somehow Kevin escaped. He booked a flight home and called me from the airport lobby."

"Did you talk with him after that?"

"Yes, briefly. This box arrived Saturday evening, and I texted him that it was here. He texted back that he had to take care of something first, but that we would meet on Sunday."

A picture of what happened was starting to emerge. He was followed back to Palm Vista by some very pissed off Russians, he met with them to negotiate a deal, and the negotiations failed. I glanced at my phone to check the time, and saw that there wasn't much of a hurry, but that I should start thinking about getting back to Palm Vista for my gig driving Samantha Gordon home.

"I don't mean to take much more of your time, but is there anything else I should know?"

He was quiet for a moment, but didn't look like he was trying to hide anything.

"I dunno. This all happened so fast. Kevin and I did business, but he was also my friend."

It was clear that Tony had told me everything of importance.

"I have a something I need to do back in Palm Vista soon, so I can't really stick around. Here's one of my cards, call me if you need me."

"Ok, the wife and I are just gonna stay here for a few weeks. I don't know what I'm supposed to do with this artifact."

Tony texted me his phone number and told me to call him if anything came up. We shook hands, and he unlocked his front door to let me out. I walked back to the car, pulled out onto the street, and was soon on the expressway heading towards Palm Vista. The drive was uneventful, and I listened to a college radio station all the way back. I was soon back in my home territory.

CHAPTER 7

I had time to grab lunch, so I decided to stop back at my apartment. I got a text message when I was a block from home, but I decided to wait on it until I was in the parking lot before I checked it. When I parked the car, I saw the message was from Colonel Gordon, reminding me to pick up Samantha at the side entrance of the school at 2pm. I responded telling him that I would do exactly that, and headed inside to my apartment to grab a bite to eat.

Since I didn't have enough time to cook anything fancy, I ended up just having some leftover pasta that had been in my fridge for days. I had to leave soon, and I was happy to be getting $500 for giving someone a lift home for a few days. Although the money was good, the situation was a bit awkward, and I hoped that this whole thing would resolve itself in the next few days. Like most things, I was just going to see how it played out.

After eating lunch, I got back in the car and began driving towards Palm Vista Academy. A few minutes later I saw something I could not believe. Right at the sidewalk in front of the school was John Bonito in a white shirt and jeans and some woman wearing a bathrobe. I immediately regretted not having tinted windows. If John Bonito saw me, there was a good chance he would recognize me from our run-in yesterday.

As I pulled into the parking lot entrance, I was relieved to see that he was staring intently towards the school building, and was not even looking in my direction. I pulled out my phone and snapped a few photos of them as I drove past. The photos looked terrible, but would help Samantha prove that she was being stalked when this inevitably went to court. Keeping an eye on John Bonito in the rearview mirror, I felt confident that he hadn't seen me.

I drove around the left part of the building and parked near the side entrance. I still had a few minutes to spare, and decided to turn the radio on. This was probably going to be an awkward car ride, and a little background music might help. A few minutes later I saw Samantha Gordon exit the side door, and I rolled down my window and leaned out.

"Samantha," I said loud enough for her to hear, but not so loud that it might spook her. She looked around for a moment and then saw where I was parked. She looked relieved to see me, and climbed into the passenger seat of the car.

"That guy is out front," I said, "I want you out of view when we drive past him, so slide down in your seat when we get close."

"Ok," she said

The scene in front of the building had changed, school was now letting out and there were lots of students heading for their cars or school bus. We were a few moments ahead of the traffic jam, and I was able to pull alongside the edge of the parking lot towards the exit onto the street. John Bonito and the woman were still standing in the exact same spot, scanning the crowds with their eyes. Samantha ducked low in her seat. At the critical moment as I drove past them, John Bonito looked directly at me through the windshield. His eyes followed me as I pulled out of the parking lot, and I saw in the rearview that he was still looking towards the car as I pulled onto the boulevard. I had been spotted, but he made no attempt to run after me.

After we were back on the main strip, I told Samantha that we were safe, and that she could sit normally in her seat. I then asked her for directions to her house, and it turned out she lived nearby. She also told me that she often walks to school.

As expected, the drive was awkward. The radio was barely helping, the station was playing a lousy song, but I didn't feel like messing with it. To make conversation, I told her that I was going to help her file an injunction against John Bonito, and that I would text her father the relevant information. I told her that when the police served him the injunction, that would probably scare him away from any further stalking. I also told her that after the restraining order was approved by the court, any further stalking would be a felony and he would go to jail. Samantha didn't really say much, but was polite and quiet.

Following her directions, I found myself making a left turn onto a street that I had driven past numerous times, but had never explored. We were still more or less in downtown Palm Vista, but suddenly the homes became much larger than I expected. This was a hidden pocket of wealth just off the main strip. Eventually we reached the Gordon house, and I told her that I would pick her up at the same spot at the same time tomorrow. She thanked me, and I waited in the car until I saw she was safely inside. After that, I decided to head back to the office to prepare whatever paperwork I was going to submit to her father.

Returning home, I spent a little time with Rory Macaw, and decided that all of his toys looked a bit chewed up and that it might be time for a new one. I added it to my list of things to do this week. I grabbed a can of soda out of the fridge, and realized that I needed a moment to clear my head before doing anything else. I put on a bit of music and sat down in my recliner. I felt stressed out, and kind of sad. It was still the middle of the afternoon, but I felt like I had already had a full day.

After hanging around the apartment for a few moments, I decided that it would be good to get the material I would be sending to the Colonel together. I had a photo of the report filed at the school, and I had a photo of John Bonito standing in front of the school. I decided to run the name John Bonito on my software to see if anything useful would pop up, and immediately discovered that the apartment belonged to a Stella Bonito, who I assumed was John's sister and may have been the woman in the bathrobe. That would also explain the women's clothes I saw when I was there yesterday. Second, John Bonito was on the sex offender registry. He was not supposed to be anywhere near a school building, and the fact that he's staying with his sister right across the street from one is certainly a matter for the police.

I texted Colonel Gordon the photo of the school incident report and the photo of him standing outside the school, which should be all that was needed to prove a pattern of repeated harassment. I took a screenshot of his sex offender page, which would help get the court's attention. I also gave him information on filing an injunction, and told him that an attorney would be helpful for the hearing. He texted back that he still wants me to drive Samantha home tomorrow, and I agreed. I debated calling the police directly about the sex offender registry, but I knew that this would all be coming out in the next couple days when they served him the restraining order. Looking at the time, I saw that it was now late in the afternoon, meaning that a judge might not be able to approve the temporary injunction until tomorrow. There is no evidence that John Bonito knew where Samantha lived, so it seemed unlikely that this would prove to be a problem.

A moment after concluding my exchange with the Colonel, my phone started ringing, and it was Julia's number.

"Hello?"

"Frank, please come over."

"What happened?"

"I just got back from my sister's and someone broke in to the house."

"I'll be right there."

I quickly put my shoes back on and hurried out to the car. There was no way this was just some random break-in. Cuiardo must still be in town, and he was looking for the object that he feels is rightfully his. This was either good or bad news. Bad because Julia might be in danger, but good because we might still be able to bust him. He should have left when he had the chance.

A few moments later I arrived at Julia's house, and she was clearly afraid. The place was not exactly turned upside down, but she showed me Kevin's office and someone had obviously been through here. The bookshelf had been disturbed and there were numerous volumes scattered on the floor. A chair was on its side, and Julia told me that his small safe had been stolen.

"We need to report this to the police," I said, and Julia agreed. I normally try not to rush to the police over every little thing, but if Julia was in danger then that was another story.

Julia dialed the police and asked for Detective Muon. She sat silent on the phone for a moment, and then seemed to be connected with the detective. She reported the break-in, and he said he would be on his way over. This was going to be awkward. I hadn't seen David Muon since the murder of one of my clients a few months ago, and I felt like he thought I was some sort of idiot.

I also had a huge decision to make. The part of me that wanted revenge on Cuiardo knew that I would have to leave the police out of this. If the cops got to him first, then he would be detained, but he might end up free again if there was insufficient evidence. If I wanted true justice, I would have to handle this on my own.

A possible plan began to form in my mind. The Cuiardo Art Gallery website had all of Matteo's contact information. Email, phone, social media, everything. I could get a message to him if I really wanted to. If he was still in Palm Vista, then I may be able to set a time and place to meet. He killed my friend Kevin, and now Julia was in danger. A deep anger welled up within me.

"What's wrong?" Julia asked.

"Nothing. Not sure if I should tell the cops everything I've found out."

"I didn't tell them you were here. You don't have to be here when they arrive."

"I need a moment to think."

I sat down on Kevin's office chair, and it was obvious that I had two paths open before me. Path one was I try to set up a meeting with Cuiardo and gun him down. He would probably have his goons with him, which would be extremely dangerous for me. I could set up a meeting and snipe him from a distance. I could probably line up a rifle, and arrange the meeting where I could set up in a nearby window. Unfortunately, I've never shot a sniper rifle, and had to be honest with myself about my lack of long-distance shooting experience. If I brought my pistol, I could try to meet them alone, but every time I pictured it I got a couple shots off before they ended up shooting me. This plan was a nice power fantasy, but would not work in real life.

The other possibility was getting the police involved. I could set up a meeting and wear a wire, get them to confess the killing and have the cops rush in. We would have the evidence to convict, and there's a chance I would survive to see another day. Nothing was going to bring Kevin back, but at least this way there was some sort of justice. I hated working with the cops, and up to this point had mostly avoided it.

"The detective might be here soon," Julia reminded me.

"I think I'm going to stay," I responded.

A few moments later a police car pulled into the driveway, and I saw Muon emerge from the car. Detective David Muon is tall and muscular, and probably had to be twice as qualified as the others to become a police detective as a black man. Julia met him at the door, and invited him inside.

"My friend Frank is here," she told him.

Detective Muon and I shook hands, and I waited for him to say something insulting to me about the death of my former client. There was an unreadable expression on his face, and he turned to face Julia.

"You say a safe was stolen?" he asked.

Julia showed him upstairs to Kevin's office, and pointed to where the safe had been located, and also pointed out that someone had clearly moved around of bunch of things. When Detective Muon returned to the living room, I told him I might have some information about Kevin's murder.

"You have a suspect?" he asked.

"Yes," I responded. "I believe that he was murdered by a man named Matteo Cuiardo over a valuable work of art."

The detective pulled out a small notebook and a pen.

"Go on," he said.

"Kevin gave the art to a friend for safekeeping, and I spoke to this friend this morning. He said that Kevin told him that some shady people from Russia were after it. I spoke to a contact at the Palm Vista Hotel, and he told me that there were some Russians staying there the night of the murder. I got the name of one of the Russians, and it turns out he's an art dealer. This man is my number one suspect."

Muon didn't say anything for a moment, and scribbled something in his notepad.

"Could you spell the name of the man for me, and also give me the name of Kevin's friend who currently has the work of art?"

I spelled Matteo Cuiardo for him, and suddenly realized that I had gotten Tony involved with the police in a way that he probably would be mad about. I would never rat anyone out to the cops, but technically Tony hadn't broken any laws. I tried to think of a way out of this situation, but it was too late.

"His friend is Tony St. Vitus, he's the guy who owns St. Vitus Pawn off the main strip."

The detective seemed to know who I was talking about.

"I found Mr. Cuiardo's contact information for his art gallery, and the fact that this break-in just occurred makes me think he's still in town. I could contact him telling him I had the artwork and set up a meeting."

Detective Muon immediately caught my drift.

"I need to clear this with the Chief," he said, "but this is something we may be able to do."

"Do you want me to contact the art gallery?"

"Hold off a while," he answered. "Let me take your info and we'll be in touch in a couple hours."

"What about Julia? Can you have one of officers keep an eye on this place?"

"I'll make sure someone is on this street for the rest of the day."

I gave him my card, and he was soon on his way back to the squad car. He stayed in the driveway for another ten minutes, probably filling out a police report. Julia looked exhausted, and I got the sense that she probably just wanted to take a nap. After the squad car pulled out to the street, I asked her if she wanted me to stay, but she said that she would be going back to her sister's house to lay down for a while. I told her I would call her later. I said my goodbyes and headed out to the car.

Not having any place else to go, I decided to head home. It was around 5pm, and I had been awake since dawn. There's not much I could do until I got the go-ahead from Detective Muon, and I felt like I had lived an entire week in the past day. I drove to the apartment, went upstairs, and climbed into bed for a moment to clear my head. I was asleep within minutes.

CHAPTER 8

I slept for three hours, and woke up feeling groggy. It was 8pm, and I couldn't believe it was still the same day as my morning visit to Tony St. Vitus's house. I turned on a few lights in the apartment, went to the kitchen and picked a few things out of the fridge. I then turned on my computer, checked my email and then browsed a few sites that I check occasionally. About twenty minutes later, my phone then started to ring, and I didn't recognize the number.

"Hello?" I answered.

"Hello. This is Detective Muon."

"Hello," I replied.

"We want you to set up that meeting."

"Ok, I'll email him right now."

"Good. Call or text me at this number if you hear anything back."

Returning to my computer, I switched on my VPN and fired up a burner email account. I copied the email address for the gallery off of its website, and stared at the blank screen for a moment while trying to think of how to word this email. I finally started typing, and told him that I had the Luwian artifact, was in Palm Vista, and would sell it to him. One of these statements wasn't true, but this man had murdered my friend and I didn't care about being upfront with him. I hit send on the email, and figured that this was all I could do for now. He might write back immediately, it might be a few hours, or I might never hear from him.

Without warning, there was a suddenly a loud banging on my side door. For a split second I didn't want to answer it, but it might just be a delivery person or one of my neighbors. I walked over and opened the door, and found myself face to face with John Bonito.

"Who are you and what the **** were you doing in my apartment yesterday?"

"I'm a Private Investigator."

I noticed that he was holding a switchblade, and knew I had to choose my words carefully.

"You have to stop stalking people," I said. "It's illegal."

"You know what else is illegal? Breaking into my apartment "

"That's true, I apologize for that. The door was hanging open and at the time I thought you had murdered my friend."

"What?"

"My friend was killed and you were the first name that came up."

John Bonito looked puzzled for a moment, and I started to wonder if he actually had killed someone.

"When was your friend killed?"

"Two nights ago."

He look relieved, but also put the knife right up to my face. "Wasn't me. Stay the **** away from me. I know your license plate, I know where you live."

He flicked the switchblade closed and started to walk away. I stood there until he was around the corner and out of sight. This guy was a psycho, but it was becoming increasing clear that he had little to nothing to do with Kevin's death.

I went back inside. I was now too full of adrenaline to resume my normal plans, and ended up just sitting in my chair for a solid fifteen minutes. After my nerves began to settle, I decided to check my email again. There was one new message. Cuiardo's art gallery.

The email read as following:

Hello, we are still in town and would like to meet. We are willing to offer $30,000 for this item. It will take some time to get the cash, please meet us tomorrow at 9pm at Martin Luther King Jr. Park.

I couldn't believe my luck. I immediately picked up my phone, and hit the number Detective Muon had called me from.

"This is Muon."

"This is Frank Howard Smith, I heard back from Cuiardo."
"What did he say?"

"He wants me to meet him tomorrow at 9pm at Martin Luther King Park."

"Alright," Muon replied. "Come by the station tomorrow morning."

"I'll try to get in touch with Tony to see if I can borrow the artifact. Should I bring a recording device?"

"We'll set you up with everything you need. Also, we need to get a statement from Mr. St. Vitus, but he wasn't at his business or his home. Could you please tell us his whereabouts or how we could reach him?"

I already felt bad giving Tony's name to the police, but telling them about his hideout was a step too far.

"Did you even try to look up his cell phone number? The man is not that hard to reach."

There was a brief pause, and I wondered if Muon was going to make a big deal about this.

"Alright. See you tomorrow morning."

The call ended, and I stood holding the phone in disbelief for a moment. Things were going completely to plan. By tomorrow night we would have Cuiardo in custody, assuming I wasn't killed. All I had to do was get a confession out of him, and the police would do the rest. The next step was getting the artifact from Tony.

I immediately called Tony, but it just rang and rang until I got his voice mail. I followed this with a quick text telling him there had been a breakthrough, and to please call me back. A couple minutes later my phone rang.

"Hello?"

"Frank, this is Tony. You called?"

"Yes. A lot has happened since earlier, and I wanted to give you an update."

"Sure, what's up?"

"Those people who killed Kevin are still in town, and I've been in contact with the police and we're setting up a bust. I'm going to wear a wire and we're going to nail them."

"Good. Those people deserve everything they've got coming to them."

"Yes. There is one catch, though. I told them I had the artifact, and that's how I got them to agree to meet with me."

There was a lengthy pause before Tony responded.

"I think I see where this is going."

"Is this ok with you?"

"I mean, I didn't even know this thing existed four days ago. Still, it could be worth a fortune."

"Tony, I hate to ask this favor of you. This is our one chance to get these guys. Also, I could talk to the detective about returning it to you afterward."

"Frank, we're both adults. We know that once the cops have this thing we'll never see it again."

"True, but if this doesn't happen now it will never happen."

Another pause, this one lasting so long I wasn't sure if I was supposed to say something else.

"Fine. This thing is probably cursed anyway. Come pick it up."

"I can have the detective call you, if that would help."

"No, leave me out of it. I hate the cops."

"Can I stop by in the morning?"

"Yeah, alright."

"See you then."

I had just taken a long nap, and had nothing else to do tonight. I watched a movie, then some videos on the internet, and eventually it was late enough that I was tired again. Thinking ahead to the morning, it seemed to make sense to get the artifact from Tony before going to the police station. I debated setting an alarm, but I doubted Tony wanted me there too early. Either way, that would be my first stop tomorrow.

CHAPTER 9

In the morning, I did my usual routine. I gave Rory Macaw a few of his special treats to go with his breakfast, and then got into the car. The drive to Tony's was uneventful, though I was in a strange mood. I couldn't stop thinking that I might be killed tonight. I tried to picture how it would all go down later, what I would say to try to get Matteo Cuiardo to admit to the murder. I guess the cops would either rush in as soon as they had what they needed, or maybe they would arrest him after I left. I would have to run through the plan with Detective Muon.

When I got to Tony's, he had the box with crystal disc on his living room table.

"Any luck deciphering these?" I asked.

"No. This is way above my pay grade. There are probably only a dozen people on Earth who could read these."

"There's a chance you'll get this back in a few weeks."

"I'm not counting on it. I took a bunch of photographs of it."

We both stared at the box. The disc was hidden under layers of bubble wrap.

"I'd rather catch Kevin's killer," said Tony, after a brief pause.

"Me too," I added.

"By the way, the cops have been leaving me voicemails and sending me texts. Do you know anything about that?"

"Look, I'm sorry. I didn't give them your number, but they're going to need a statement from you eventually. This is a murder investigation."

Tony seemed a little pissed off, but I don't know how else I was supposed to have handled this. He picked up the box and handed it to me, and then wished me luck on tonight's show-down. I thanked him and was soon heading back to my car. After a few now-familiar turns, I was on my way back to Palm Vista.

I debated stopping home to stash the artifact somewhere safe, but instead I decided to go straight to the police station. I felt like the odds of someone robbing my car in a police station parking lot was pretty slim. When I arrived, I locked the car and made my way inside the station and asked to see Detective Muon. The detective soon came out to greet me, and invited me to his office. I took a seat and he explained the plan.

"When you get to Martin Luther King Park, there's going to be an unmarked van, two squad cars, and several plainclothes officers there."

He slid something that looked like a thumb drive across the desk.

"This is a recording device with a transmitter," he continued. "Keep it in a pocket, but not under more than one layer of clothes."

"Alright," I answered. "Is there a plan for what I'm supposed to say, or should I improvise?"

"We need them talking," said Muon. "We're going to arrest them for the purchase of stolen goods either way, and we also have the right to detain them as suspects for the break-in at the McCake's house. You need to get us something we can use in court. Any statement that they knew Mr. McCake, that they traveled here just for the artifact, anything you get them to say will be helpful."

"I understand," I said.

"If we don't get a confession from them, we don't have a murder case. Be at the park by 9pm, and we'll do the rest."

I took the thumb drive transmitter and slid it into my pocket, and told Muon that I would get the confession. He wished me luck, and I was soon walking back out to my car. It was time to head back to the apartment.

On the drive home, it suddenly occurred to me that I might need to make arrangements for someone to take care of Rory if I ended up getting murdered. The first thing I did when I was back at my place was text Julia that I would be leaving the side door of my office unlocked, in case something happened. I still the had the whole day ahead of me, and my only obligation was round two of driving Samantha Gordon home. I had no idea if I would even still be alive tomorrow, so there was no point in running errands.

I opened the box with the artifact, and just stared at it for about five minutes. It seemed pretty solid and heavy, and as long as I didn't drop it, it could probably be handled safely. I didn't recognize any of the symbols carved into it, except one that looked like a boot and one that looked like a cow's head. Tony said it was from the Luwian culture, and I decided to go on-line and see what I could learn about them.

After reading a few pages, I realized that they were some sort of a lost civilization that had been rediscovered just in the past century. They were from what was then called Anatolia, modern-day Turkiye, and they had been there since the middle Bronze Age. They were Indo-European, and may have been one of the first migrations from Eurasia into the Middle East that had ever occurred. They pre-dated the Hittites, the Mycenaeans, and all the other Indo-Europeans. One of the websites said that ancient Troy of the Trojan War may have spoken the Luwian language, and that the Luwians survived the Bronze Age Collapse and existed until around the 7th century BC.

There was lots of photos of Luwian hieroglyphs on pottery and stone, and they looked identical to the markings on the crystal wheel in front of me. It was soon clear that there were only a few experts who could read Luwian. I took out my phone and snapped about three dozen photos of the artifact, carefully turning it over to get the markings on the reverse. I was extremely curious about what these symbols meant, and I debated contacting an expert right away. I decided that it would be best not to draw a lot of attention to the artifact until this evening's business was concluded. Word of the discovery might spread like wildfire, and I didn't want any complications.

It was nearing the time that I was supposed to pick up Samantha Gordon at school, though I still had a bit of time. Despite my trip out to Tony's and my visit to the police station, it was only the early afternoon. I grabbed a quick bite to eat, and then headed out to the car to drive over to Palm Vista Academy. When I pulled into the school's parking lot, I was relieved that John Bonito was not out front today. I met Samantha at the same spot at yesterday, and she was soon sitting in my passenger seat.

"John Bonito isn't out front today, so no need to hide."

"That's good".

There was a bit of student traffic near the exit of the parking lot, but we were soon on the main strip heading towards her house. I tried turning on the radio, but once again there was nothing good playing. I decided to try a bit of conversation.

"So...belong to any clubs at school?"

"Yes, drama club. Also, volleyball is starting up soon."

"What play are you doing this year?"

"All's Well That Ends Well."

"Is the director doing anything unusual with it, setting it in the modern day or anything?"

"She's doing everything unusual. Did you know she doesn't even want us to memorize the lines?"

"What?"

"She says the text is just a guideline. She said if we just read the written text then the play is nothing more than warmed-up leftovers."

"Huh. Normally people insist on the original dialogue."

"I dunno. It's kind of fun. She actually yelled at one of the kids for going an entire scene without improvising anything."

"What happens if you improvise so much that the plot moves in a different direction?"

"She wants us to know the plot well enough so that we can improvise without changing the final act."

"That's a new one."

I considered extending the conversation by asking her about the volleyball team, but we were about to turn down her street, and I didn't think there was time.

"My dad says they're serving that guy a restraining order later today or tonight. My dad is friends with one of the judges."

"That's great. I'll have to talk to him to see if we still need to do this ride thing tomorrow."

"Yeah, I'm not sure."

I pulled into the Gordon family's driveway, and Samantha hopped out of the car. She thanked me for the lift home, and I waited until she was in the house before leaving. I was still feeling jittery about tonight's meeting with Cuiardo, and decided to just head back to the apartment.

CHAPTER 10

The rest of the day passed quickly, and it was soon dusk. I didn't leave the house until around 7pm. It was still too early to go to the meeting spot, but my nerves were bad and I needed to get out of the apartment. On the way out, I paused for a moment to make sure I had everything I needed. In addition to the transmitter that Muon had given me, I also brought a small recorder that looked like a keyfob for a car. After some reflection, I decided to grab my gun, though I would probably end up leaving it in the car.

I left my apartment wondering if I would ever see it again. These men might be planning to kill me and take the artifact, I really had no idea what to expect. Either way, I was going to have the police there, and they might be able to reach me in time if things started to go wrong.

I decided to hit a bar near Martin Luther King Jr. park and get a drink or two. I'm not a heavy drinker, but I was feeling incredibly wound up, and my tension might be suspicious to Cuiardo. The detective told me that he would have everything in place, all I had to do was show up and try to get Cuiardo to implicate himself.

The bar I went to was called Stella's, which was right across the street from Martin Luther King Jr. Park, and luckily I was able to find a parking spot right near the entrance. As I got out of the car, I took a moment to survey the area, and try to form a plan for the meeting. The park wasn't that large, just a couple acres with a fountain and art installation in the middle, but not much else. There were a few benches scattered throughout, and I figured that if I was sitting on one with the package clearly in view, Cuiardo would have no problem finding me. I still had over an hour, so I walked into the bar and ordered a beer. I found a table off to the side, I didn't really feel like socializing, but it was nice to have people around. Stella's was not crowded, it was a Tuesday night, and the jukebox was playing some blues-rock playlist that had a few decent tracks. A waitress came over to the table after another ten minutes, and I ordered a refill on my drink.

I sat there thinking about the last few days, but my mind kept wandering back to Samantha Gordon and John Bonito, and I began to wonder if he was being served his injunction as I sat here. She said that her dad was friends with a judge, and that everything would be taken care of this evening. I might still have to drive Samantha home from school again tomorrow, but that might be the end of that job.

When the waitress brought the second beer, I also put in an order for wings, not because I was hungry, but because I knew I had some time to kill. The food arrived twenty minutes later, and I debated ordering a third beer, but I didn't think it would be smart. I took my time finishing the wings, and eventually felt like I had waited here long enough. I checked the time, and even though it was still too early, I decided that it was time to go. I paid my bill, and exited Stella's out onto the street. It was still chilly outside, and I had a moment of regret about leaving the bar. I went out to my car and retrieved the box with the artifact, and then walked into the park. I picked a bench by the art installation and sat down with the package by my side. At this point, it was just a matter of waiting.

Looking around, I saw one squad car parked at the corner of the park, a white utility van half a block down, and there was some guy with a Marlins jersey on the next bench over who looked exactly like a cop. I didn't see the second squad car or anyone else who looked undercover, but they were probably nearby. All I had to do was make the sale, get Cuiardo talking, and then leave.

Nine o'clock came and went, and there was no sign of Cuiardo. The temperature began to drop, and I was glad I brought my gray coat instead of a sweater. I tried to think of the last time there was a cold snap like this in Florida, and it had been at least a decade. I had the transmitter Muon gave me and my own recording device in the coat's right pocket, and I began to wonder if my coat was going to mess up the audio quality. I took out my recorder and slid it into my pants pocket. It suddenly occurred to me that Cuiardo may be watching me, and that I may have just done something suspicious. I looked around, but there was no sign of anyone except the guy in the Marlins jersey, and a few people over near the restaurants and bars at the edge of the park.

Without warning, the squad car turned on its lights and started blaring its siren. It peeled out onto the street, disappearing around the corner. This was alarming, as I actually felt a lot better with that car there. The man in the Marlins jersey answered his phone and began to run to the south end of the park.

I started to feel panic rush through my body. The white utility van turned on its headlights, and also left. In the distance, I could hear something that sounded like an ambulance.

Before I could process what was happening, I saw three men approaching from the north side of the park, and one of them looked in my direction. They began heading towards me. One man walked ahead of the others. He had slicked back hair and was wearing an expensive looking overcoat. I guessed that this was Cuiardo, and his face was unreadable as he approached where I was seated. Behind him, one of the men was wearing a puffy Miami Heat athletic jacket that looked like it was from the 90s, and the other guy looked under-dressed for the cold in a gray hooded sweater and gray sweatpants. The guy in the Miami Heat jacket had a black backpack slung over one shoulder, and I could tell that the sweatpants guy had a gun tucked in behind him. Cuiardo was a slender man with a thin face, and looked far more sophisticated than the other two.

"Are you here about the package?" I asked, trying to sound casual. I was still spooked by the sudden departure of all the police that were supposed to be my backup. It occurred to me that Cuiardo may have been behind the police's sudden disappearance.

"Yes," answered Cuiardo, with an obvious Russian accent, while one of the men set the backpack at my feet. "May I look in the box?"

"Sure," I answered. Cuiardo opened the lid of the box and seemed pleased. I unzipped the backpack, and it was stuffed with racks of twenties. I riffled through them, and it appeared to be about $30,000. Things were going too smoothly, and I still needed a confession out of Cuiardo.

"What is that thing?" I asked, figuring it would sound like normal conversation. Cuiardo didn't answer right away, and had an annoyed look on his face. He clearly thought I had broken some sort of unspoken protocol.

"It's something that rightfully belongs to me," he said. "Something that was stolen."

"This was given to me by a guy who was scared for his life, he didn't tell me much about it. He gave me your name and said you would probably buy it."

I was trying to act like I didn't know any better, but I hadn't gotten Cuiardo to admit the crime and I needed to keep the conversation going. I tried to think of some annoying people I had met, and figured I'd try acting like they act. Someone bothersome, but not someone you want to kill. Cuiardo seemed aggravated, and clearly thought our business was concluded.

"Your friend need not have worried, we are reasonable men. The person responsible for the theft has been taken care of, and your friend was never in danger. I believe we are finished here."

One of the men took the box, and the three of them began walking away. I wasn't sure if what Cuiardo had said would be enough for a conviction. I had made a mess of the whole thing. Where had the police vanished to? How had Cuiardo gotten them to leave? I watched helplessly as the three men disappeared into the distance. I sat for moment with the backpack filled with money, hoping to see a police car pulling up to arrest the men. Instead, all I heard was the blare of sirens in the far distance. I picked up the backpack and went back to the car. I had no idea whether to go home or go to the police station.

Once in the car, I pulled out my expensive radio receiver that could pick up emergency channels, even the encrypted ones, and what I heard over the airwaves was shocking. Several police officers were dead, more injured. There was an active shooter. I continued to listen, but it was just a series of frantic calls for assistance. The EMS could not go on the scene until the shooter had been neutralized, and police officers were bleeding to death. One of the 911 operators gave the location of the shooting to a neighboring town's police department, and I quickly looked the address up on my phone. It was the apartment tower across from the Palm Vista Academy.

John Bonito. He was being served his injunction tonight. I tried to tell myself that there were other possibilities, but the timing was undeniable. I tried to think of how Cuiardo may have pulled this off, but I also wondered if this was just a coincidence. Why would a Russian art dealer have anything to do with some psycho who lived in town? The timing could not have been worse.

I turned the ignition, and just sat there in my car. The police station was going to be crazy right now, so I decided to drive back to my apartment. There was no point driving down Main Street, since it was going to be blocked off, so I took a few side streets. When I got back to my building, I grabbed the backpack full of money, and then went upstairs and turned on the news.

There were reporters on the scene, and the apartment tower was surrounded by about thirty cop cars, two SWAT vans, a dozen ambulance, and even a few random fire trucks. The reporter said that there were six confirmed casualties. They showed a photo of John Bonito. A few minutes later, there was footage of John Bonito being wheeled out on a stretcher by two paramedics. He was covered in blood, and his face was covered with a breathing apparatus. I couldn't see any movement of his hands or any other part of his body. He looked dead.

CHAPTER 11

Detective Muon was killed in the line of duty, along with two other police officers. Five other officers were wounded, but were expected to survive. The incident dominated the national news, and was even covered on international channels. It was painful seeing David Muon's photo over and over, as well as the two other officers. I felt a tremendous sense of guilt about what happened, even though I never planned for any of this. It was supposed to be a routine serving of a restraining order, like the thousands of restraining orders that are served every day. If I had never moved to Palm Vista, none of this ever would have happened. I tried to comfort myself that I may have saved Samantha from an eventual attack from John Bonito, but that was all speculation.

I didn't hear from the cops until two days later. A detective called me, but he only asked me about the events at Martin Luther King Jr. Park. I told him a short version of what had happened after his men had left. I still had their transmitter shaped like a thumb drive, and had also recorded the whole conversation with Cuiardo on my keyfob recorder. He asked me to drop both of these and the backpack full of money off at the station. I told him I would be by later that day.

The detective who inherited the Kevin McCake murder case introduced himself as Detective Sanchez, and he asked me if the recording device contained an admission of guilt by Cuiardo. I told him that it was incriminating, but fell short of a full confession. I gave him the listening device, the recorder, and then the backpack. He told me that the backpack and keyfob would be stored in the evidence locker, and that he would put my name on the tag for both of them. I knew I would never see either of them again.

It seemed like the police had lost interest in the Kevin McCake murder. The detective told me that the recordings would be given to the District Attorney, and that it was up to the FBI at this point to find Cuiardo. I asked him to call me if there were any developments, but I could tell by his reaction that it would be unlikely that I would hear from him. I would probably have to call the DA's office if I wanted any updates. If I had known how badly the sting operation would have gone, so badly that it arguably didn't even happen, I never would have gotten the police involved. My friend's murderer was right in front of me, and instead of gunning him down I handed him a priceless artifact. I was still planning on getting back at Cuiardo, but revenge now involved flying to Moscow. I comforted myself that maybe Cuiardo would be extradited and face charges, but I knew that it was unlikely.

Kevin's funeral was the next Saturday. Closed casket wake, then a church service the next morning before the funeral. I never knew Kevin's family was Catholic, and they somehow lined up the cathedral for the mass. The whole ceremony is now a blur in my memory, but I remember they played "In Paradiso" as the pallbearers carried the casket down the aisle. I didn't recognize most of the people there, they were probably family and people from the academy. Julia looked stunned the entire time.

The funeral was rough. It was still colder than usual for January, but the sun was shining. After they lowered the coffin into the ground, I said my final goodbyes and headed home.

Later that night, I turned on the television and was stunned to see an interview John Bonito's sister. She was wearing an absurd amount of make-up, and was clearly insane. She blamed the police for harassing her brother, and said that John was just acting in self-defense. Something about her eyes reminded me of a cult member, I think she idolized her brother. She said that she was praying for his speedy recovery.

John Bonito was shot seven times, and was in critical condition at Miami General. The whole nation was waiting for news of his death, but it never happened. I worried that I would be pulled into this mess eventually, and I'm sure Colonel Gordon and his daughter probably had to give a statement. I kept waiting for the phone to ring, but it seemed that my role in this had been forgotten.

Over the next few months, I followed John Bonito's trial with great interest. His lawyers had him plead insanity, and the prosecutors were pushing for the death penalty. He was convicted and sentenced to death. He appealed the decision, and the whole thing might take a year or two to resolve. They don't exactly execute people the week after a verdict.

I never heard another word about Matteo Cuiardo from the police. I debated calling the DA a few times, but I felt like there was no point. The half-confession I got on the recording device probably wasn't enough to extradite someone from Russia. I replayed that evening at Martin Luther King park over and over in my imagination, trying to think of different things I could have said or done to get the confession. Cuiardo was not the type to slip up, and there probably was nothing I could have done differently.

Things started to return to normal. I kept up with Julia somewhat infrequently, and had the feeling that my presence reminded her of her loss. I also never got the backpack filled with money back from the evidence locker. I did ask about it one time, but was told that the investigation was still ongoing.

Once a week, I would type the name Cuiardo into a search engine, and also search for any news about the crystal disc with the Luwian writing. It's been a few months, and other than Cuiardo's art gallery holding events occasionally, I haven't found much. The fate of the artifact has remained a mystery. It remains unclear whether Cuiardo himself was the Russian financing the dig in Switzerland, or if he was working for someone else.

The whole incident was beginning to recede into my memory when something unexpected happened. I opened my email and had a message from TRULINC, the Florida prison system email service. This was odd, because I had only signed up for TRULINC to communicate with a former client of mine, but that case was long closed. I opened the email, and wasn't prepared for what it said.

Mr. Frank Howard Smith,

Bet your surprised to hear from me! I am writing to apologize for thretening you with a knife. Part of my recovary is contacting people I have wronged. I'm sorry.

-John Bonito

There was no way I was going to respond to this email. At this point I no longer considered him a suspect in Kevin's murder, but I've learned the hard way not engage with psychopaths. I closed out the email and hoped that I never heard from him again. The next week I got another email from him.

Mr. Frank Howard Smith,

I owe you another apology. You broke into my apartment and caused me to get all my guns out of storage. I blamed you for what happened, since none of it would have happened if I hadn't got the guns. I have been talking with my pastor and I was wrong. I'm sorry.

-John Bonito

A few weeks later he sent me a rambling email about life in prison. He then sent me another lengthy email talking about his church group at the prison, and what a blessing they have been for him. He kept sending me emails every few weeks. Eventually I caved, and wrote to him that I forgave him, but to stop contacting me. I regretted this as soon as I hit send. If I had never responded, he probably would have just assumed my TRULINC

account was inactive. After that, the emails became more fre-
quent. I made a point to never write back to him again, though I
did read all the messages he sent me.

One morning, I was drinking a cup of coffee and reading a
chapter from a prison memoir from the 19th century. The book
talked about how terrible prisons were at this time, and it got me
thinking about the prison system and how they operate. It also
discussed how prisons used to attract tourists, who would pay
a small fee to get a tour of the facilities. This struck me as sort
of odd, although touring a prison probably would give someone
a decent amount of perspective. I decided that maybe I would
watch something on prisons later, since it seemed like an interesting topic.

After finishing the chapter, I went over to my computer to
check my email. There was a new message from John Bonito.

Mr. Frank Howard Smith,

Florida State Prison is having a visitors day next Friday. There
will be snacks and the cafeteria will be decorated. I know you are
mad but please visit me. The only person I ever see is my sister. I
already gave them your name as a possible visitor. Everything will
be ok if you show up.

-John Bonito

I had no desire to ever see John Bonito again, and wished that
he would stop writing me. I hate existing in this man's mind, and

the fact that he seems to think about me a lot makes me uncomfortable. I am not friends with him, and every encounter I've had with him has been terrible. Still, it's odd that I was just thinking about visiting a prison when this email arrived. Watching a documentary is one thing, but seeing one in real life would probably satisfy my curiosity for good. On the other hand, if I did visit John Bonito, I would never get rid of him. Ignoring him seemed like the smart thing to do.

Going to bed that next Thursday evening, I had resolved not to visit the prison the next day. It was hours away, I didn't even like John Bonito, and he was one of the most hated men in the entire country. If anyone got the idea that I was friends with John Bonito, my reputation would be forever tarnished.

Friday morning, I awoke from an extremely vivid dream that I had gone to visit Florida State Prison. It wasn't even a nightmare, it was one of those dreams where everything feels real. John Bonito wasn't in the dream, I just was at the prison on some sort of tour. I remember the tour guide was quite unusual, and was cracking jokes the entire time. This dream left me in an unusual frame of mind, as I have a habit of taking dreams seriously. If I dream that someone is bad news, I try to avoid them for awhile. If I have a dream that I watch a certain movie, I try to watch that movie in the coming days. Also, if the dream is dark or weird, I don't take it seriously. I would never do something bad just because of a dream.

Florida State Prison was way up north. I had decided earlier that I wasn't going to go, but a few days ago I did look up the visiting hours, and knew that they were between 1pm and 4pm. It would be hard to describe what I was thinking, but I found myself seriously debating going there this afternoon. I really didn't have any major plans today, and after breakfast I sat in my recliner for a long time trying to talk myself out of the trip. It made no logical sense, I didn't feel like interacting with a psycho today, and also it was kind of a far drive. On the other hand, I couldn't get that dream out of my mind.

I decided to go. Call me superstitious, but I was planning on watching something on prisons tonight anyways, so why not go see a real prison. If I left now, I would make it well before the visiting hours ended. I grabbed a few bottles of water and can of cola out of the fridge, and figured I'd probably hit a drive-thru at some point. I went out to the car and turned the ignition, and was soon turning on the main street towards the expressway. I made only one stop on the way, a rest stop about halfway, and turned off Route 95 a little before Jacksonville. Another hour on a few state roads heading west and then north, and I found myself approaching an arched gate welcoming me to the prison. Ahead of me was an industrial looking building that was surrounded by a high barbed wire fence. There was a large parking area, and I pulled into a spot and made my way to the entrance.

Pushing open the doors, I found myself in a small waiting room with a woman behind what appeared to be bullet-proof glass, with small holes for speaking through. I told her I was here to visit inmate John Bonito. She asked me for my ID and told me to take a seat. When she called my name again, it was only to return my ID. A few minutes later, a prison guard opened the steel door at the end of the room.

"Visitor for John Bonito?"

I stood up, and the man motioned that I should follow him. We walked down a drab hallway towards what looked like a cafeteria. Tacked up on the wall were shiny letters spelling out the word "Welcome" and a long table with sandwiches and drinks. I noticed that there were about ten prison guards standing around the perimeter, all with holstered firearms. There were about twenty small tables that were covered with shiny reflective tablecloths, and groups of both civilians and people wearing orange jumpsuits were already seated around six or seven of the tables. I would not describe the atmosphere as festive, but someone had at least put in a little effort.

Looking around the room, I didn't see John Bonito anywhere. I took a seat at one of the empty tables, and after a short wait I saw John enter the room flanked by two prison guards. I gestured broadly that I was the visitor, and the two prison guards guided him towards the table and then left.

"Mr. Frank Howard Smith!"

I was surprised at his composure, he seemed like a different person than last time I saw him.

"Hello, John. Surprised to see me?"

"Yes and no," he answered.

"How's the treatment in this place?" I asked, trying to break the ice.

"Could be worse," he responded. "I'm glad you came today. My church group says that it's better to apologize to someone in person."

"It's ok," I said. I debated telling him that his killing spree messed up my chances to bring Kevin's murderer to justice, but I didn't feel like talking about it. There was an awkward moment of silence, and I wasn't sure what to say. John looked around the room, and seemed satisfied about something,

"This place really isn't so bad. If you had a great life on the outside it's a big step down, but for a guy like me it isn't so bad."

"I guess it's three meals a day and a roof over your head."

"Yes, it's not so bad because I actually deserve worse than this. There are guys here who are innocent, and it's terrible for them. For me, it isn't so bad."

"I'd still like to stay out of places like this if I can help it."

"The best part is the people I've met. My life is completely different now."

I felt a bit disoriented. Prisons are terrible places, and I deeply dislike how prisons have become profit-oriented enterprises. Private prisons make a fortune charging taxpayers $40,000 per inmate while only spending $10,000, not to mention the forced labor. Yet here is a man celebrating being in prison.

"You wouldn't rather be on the outside?" I asked, after a moment.

"Yes, someday, but this will always be the place where I met Jesus Christ."

"Found God while locked up, huh?"

"I've repented of my sins, and they've been forgiven me."

I suddenly felt angry. This was the cold-blooded murderer who killed Detective Muon and the others. It had been an enormous mistake coming here today. I decided to stay only another minute, and then head out.

"How many people did you kill?"

John paused for a moment, counting in his head.

"Four people. Three cops, and one person previously."

I decided that the fastest way out of this situation without seeming rude was to grab some snacks from the table, and when I was done eating I could leave. I felt stupid for thinking that I'd be seeing the entire prison today, this was a long drive just to sit in a cafeteria. I asked John if he wanted anything from the refreshment table, and he asked me to grab him a soda. When I returned to the table, there was a long silence.

"Frank, while I've been here I've joined a church."

"That's great," I said. I didn't mean to sound sarcastic, but I could hear it in my own voice.

"I'm serious," he continued. "Jesus created our entire reality. This whole universe is just something he created."

I wasn't sure how to respond to this change in John Bonito. I was in no mood for a lecture from the man who killed all those people, but I also marveled at the idea that maybe John Bonito was on a genuine path towards some sort of rehabilitation.

"Jesus loves you, Frank. It doesn't matter who we were, or what we did. Anyone who approaches him with a repentant heart will be forgiven."

I quickly ate my brownie and downed my drink. The flash of anger I experienced a few moments ago had passed. I didn't feel any hate for John Bonito, he's just someone who doesn't belong on the outside, that's all.

"John, I'm glad I came today, but I can't stay much longer."

He looked disappointed that I was leaving.

"I wanted to give you the gospel, Frank. It's the least I could do."

He gestured with his arm towards our surroundings.

"This is all an emanation from Jesus, Frank. This prison, your whole life. He took the execution that we deserved. We are free men now, the charges have been dropped. After the lethal injection, I will be with him face to face."

I had forgotten about the death sentence. I stood up, but felt like I should say something before I left.

"Take care, John. I'm glad I came today."

He looked like he wanted me to stay, and was clearly thinking of some way to get me to sit down again. He thanked me for coming, and I started to make my way back to the hallway. I didn't have any trouble from the guards as I turned towards the exit, and was buzzed through the door back into the entrance room. After signing out with the woman behind the glass partition, I was exiting the prison back into the fresh air. Looking up, I noticed that it was one of those afternoons where the moon is visible in the sky. The prison was a barren, brutalist place, and I couldn't wait to get home. I still had a long drive ahead of me. I got in the car, drove through the arch outside of the prison parking lot, and felt like some era of my life had just ended.

CHAPTER 12

About The Author

Robert Grenier lives in Rochester, NY. His previous books include the neo-fantasy novel <u>It Could All Be A Dream</u>, and a novelette called <u>The Adventures of Commodore</u>.

Thank you for reading Night Shock!

Printed in the USA
CPSIA information can be obtained
at www.ICGtesting.com
CBHW051004051024
15373CB00050B/1897

9 798330 383092